Shadow
of the Shark

Magic Tree House® Books

#1: Dinosaurs Before Dark
#2: The Knight at Dawn
#3: Mummies in the Morning
#4: Pirates Past Noon
#5: Night of the Ninjas
#6: Afternoon on the Amazon
#7: Sunset of the Sabertooth
#8: Midnight on the Moon
#9: Dolphins at Daybreak
#10: Ghost Town at Sundown
#11: Lions at Lunchtime
#12: Polar Bears Past Bedtime
#13: Vacation Under the Volcano
#14: Day of the Dragon King
#15: Viking Ships at Sunrise
#16: Hour of the Olympics
#17: Tonight on the *Titanic*
#18: Buffalo Before Breakfast
#19: Tigers at Twilight
#20: Dingoes at Dinnertime
#21: Civil War on Sunday
#22: Revolutionary War on Wednesday
#23: Twister on Tuesday
#24: Earthquake in the Early Morning
#25: Stage Fright on a Summer Night
#26: Good Morning, Gorillas
#27: Thanksgiving on Thursday
#28: High Tide in Hawaii

Merlin Missions

#29: Christmas in Camelot
#30: Haunted Castle on Hallows Eve
#31: Summer of the Sea Serpent
#32: Winter of the Ice Wizard
#33: Carnival at Candlelight
#34: Season of the Sandstorms
#35: Night of the New Magicians
#36: Blizzard of the Blue Moon
#37: Dragon of the Red Dawn
#38: Monday with a Mad Genius
#39: Dark Day in the Deep Sea
#40: Eve of the Emperor Penguin
#41: Moonlight on the Magic Flute
#42: A Good Night for Ghosts
#43: Leprechaun in Late Winter
#44: A Ghost Tale for Christmas Time
#45: A Crazy Day with Cobras
#46: Dogs in the Dead of Night

#47: Abe Lincoln at Last!
#48: A Perfect Time for Pandas
#49: Stallion by Starlight
#50: Hurry Up, Houdini!
#51: High Time for Heroes
#52: Soccer on Sunday

Super Editions

Danger in the Darkest Hour

Magic Tree House® Fact Trackers

Dinosaurs
Knights and Castles
Mummies and Pyramids
Pirates
Rain Forests
Space
Titanic
Twisters and Other Terrible Storms
Dolphins and Sharks
Ancient Greece and the Olympics
American Revolution
Sabertooths and the Ice Age
Pilgrims
Ancient Rome and Pompeii
Tsunamis and Other Natural Disasters
Polar Bears and the Arctic
Sea Monsters
Penguins and Antarctica
Leonardo da Vinci
Ghosts
Leprechauns and Irish Folklore
Rags and Riches: Kids in the Time of Charles Dickens
Snakes and Other Reptiles
Dog Heroes
Abraham Lincoln
Pandas and Other Endangered Species
Horse Heroes
Heroes for All Times
Soccer
Ninjas and Samurai
 China: Land of the Emperor's Great Wall
Sharks and Other Predators

More Magic Tree House®

Games and Puzzles from the Tree House
Magic Tricks from the Tree House
My Magic Tree House Journal
Magic Tree House Survival Guide
Animal Games and Puzzles

MAGIC TREE HOUSE® #53
A MERLIN MISSION

Shadow of the Shark

by Mary Pope Osborne

illustrated by Sal Murdocca

A STEPPING STONE BOOK™

Random House 🏠 New York

Text copyright © 2015 by Mary Pope Osborne
Jacket art and interior illustrations copyright © 2015 by Sal Murdocca

Visit us on the Web!
SteppingStonesBooks.com
MagicTreeHouse.com

Educators and librarians, for a variety of teaching tools, visit us at
RHTeachersLibrarians.com

Library of Congress Cataloging-in-Publication Data
Osborne, Mary Pope.
Shadow of the shark / Mary Pope Osborne ; illustrated by Sal Murdocca. — First edition.
pages cm. — (Magic Tree House ; #53)
Summary: As a thank-you from Merlin and Morgan, Jack and Annie are sent on what should be a vacation at a luxurious resort in Cozumel, Mexico, but is, by mistake, an adventure with ancient Mayans, instead.
ISBN 978-0-553-51081-2 (trade) — ISBN 978-0-553-51082-9 (lib. bdg.) — ISBN 978-0-553-51083-6 (ebook)
[1. Time travel—Fiction. 2. Adventure and adventurers—Fiction. 3. Magic—Fiction. 4. Mayas—Fiction. 5. Indians of Central America—Fiction. 6. Brothers and sisters—Fiction. 7. Cozumel Island (Mexico)—History—Fiction. 8. Yucatán Peninsula—History—Fiction.] I. Murdocca, Sal, illustrator. II. Title.
PZ7.O81167Sh 2015 [Fic]—dc23 2015000502

Printed in the United States of America
10 9 8 7 6 5 4 3 2 1
First Edition

This book has been officially leveled by using the F&P Text Level Gradient™ Leveling System.

For Cindy Mill,
with gratitude

CONTENTS

Prologue

One summer day in Frog Creek, Pennsylvania, a mysterious tree house appeared in the woods. It was filled with books. A boy named Jack and his sister, Annie, found the tree house and soon discovered that it was magic. They could go to any time and place in history just by pointing to a picture in one of the books. While they were gone, no time at all passed back in Frog Creek.

Jack and Annie eventually found out that the tree house belonged to Morgan le Fay, a magical librarian from the legendary realm of Camelot. They have since traveled on many adventures in the magic tree house and completed many missions for both Morgan le Fay and her friend Merlin the magician. Teddy and Kathleen, two young enchanters from Camelot, have sometimes helped Jack and Annie in both big and small ways.

Now Jack and Annie will use the magic tree house to go on a new kind of mission. . . .

CHAPTER ONE

Dream Vacation

"Did you see anything amazing?" Annie asked Jack. They were standing on the warm, sunny shore of Frog Creek Lake, packing up their new swimming gear—flippers, masks, snorkels, and red life vests.

"Not really," said Jack. "Weeds and rocks."

"Same here," said Annie. "How was your new mask?"

"Cool," said Jack as he put his glasses back on. "It didn't leak or fog up at all."

"Great," said Annie, pulling a tunic over her bathing suit.

Jack and Annie stepped into their flip-flops. Jack picked up the waterproof swim bag with all their gear, and they headed to the bike rack. "I'd love to snorkel around a coral reef someday," he said.

"Me too!" said Annie.

Jack strapped the bulky bag to the rack over his back wheel. He and Annie pulled on their helmets and pedaled out of the lake parking lot.

"Remember when Randy and Jenny snorkeled around a coral reef last spring?" Jack said.

"Oh, right, they went to a place called Cozumel with their parents," Annie said. "They did all kinds of cool stuff. Hey, should we call them? They said they'd be back from their aunt's house by two."

"Sure," said Jack.

"Hold on, stop," said Annie.

Jack and Annie pulled their bikes over to the side of the quiet road. Annie reached into her handlebar bag and took out the old cell phone their dad had given them when he had gotten a newer model. "Hey, we have a text from Randy." She read the message. "Darn. He says they're not coming back until tomorrow."

"That's okay. Let's just go home, then," said Jack. He started pedaling again and turned at the corner. He started up their street, heading for their house.

"Jack, stop!" Annie called from behind him.

Jack stopped his bike and looked back. Annie was speeding after him. "What's wrong?" he called.

She screeched to a halt. "We have a message from Teddy!" she cried, waving a yellow piece of paper. "When I put the phone away, I noticed this in my handlebar bag!"

"How did it get there?" said Jack.

"I don't know!" said Annie. "Teddy must have put it there when we were snorkeling! Or maybe when my bike was in our yard or parked at the library! Or maybe—"

"Okay, okay, just read it to me," said Jack.

"Jack stopped his bike and looked back."

Annie read breathlessly:

Jack and Annie,
   Please meet me at the tree house
as soon as possible.

                              Teddy

"Let's go!" said Jack.

Annie put the message back in the bag, and she and Jack sped up the street. When they reached the edge of the Frog Creek woods, they turned and rode their bikes between the trees, bouncing over roots, pine needles, and leaves.

"Teddy hasn't come to Frog Creek in a long time!" said Annie.

"I know!" said Jack.

"I hope nothing's wrong back in Camelot!" said Annie. "I hope Morgan and Merlin are all right."

"Yeah, and Kathleen!" said Jack.

"And Penny!" said Annie. "And Arthur—and, well, all of Camelot!"

Jack and Annie soon came to the tallest oak.

The magic tree house was back. A freckle-faced teenager with tousled red hair was leaning out of the window.

"Teddy!" Annie cried, waving.

"Hello!" he called. "Climb on up!"

Annie and Jack pulled off their helmets, left their bikes leaning against the tree, and climbed up the rope ladder. Inside the tree house, they both hugged Teddy.

"What's happening?" said Jack. "Is everyone okay?"

"Oh, yes! Camelot is doing quite well," said Teddy.

"Good," said Annie.

"Do Merlin and Morgan have a new mission for us?" said Jack.

"Indeed they do!" said Teddy.

"What do they want us to do?" asked Annie.

"They want you to have a fantastic time," said Teddy.

"What does that mean?" said Jack.

"Merlin and Morgan believe they have never properly thanked you for all your hard and dangerous work," said Teddy.

"Oh, sure they have," said Annie. "They always thank us."

Teddy smiled. "Well, today they want to thank you in a very special way: they want to send you on a holiday."

"A holiday? You mean like a vacation?" said Jack.

"Yes, a vacation. I believe that's what you call it," said Teddy.

"Oh, man, we were just talking about that," said Jack.

"Wonderful!" said Teddy. "Then their timing is perfect. The question is: where would you most like to go?"

"Well, we were just talking about a place called Cozumel," said Annie.

"Cozumel?" said Teddy. "I do not believe I have heard of that land."

"It's an island in the Caribbean Sea, next to the Yucatán Peninsula," said Jack. "It's part of Mexico."

"We want to go there because it's a great place for snorkeling," said Annie.

"Snorkeling?" said Teddy, wrinkling his nose. "What is that?"

Jack laughed. "You swim in a lake or ocean and look underwater through a mask."

"And breathe through a plastic tube," said Annie.

"Our lake isn't great for snorkeling," said Jack. "But our friends Randy and Jenny went to a beach in Cozumel last spring, and they said the snorkeling was incredible."

"Ah, I see. Then Cozumel is where you shall go," said Teddy. He reached into his cloak and pulled out a wand. He waved it in a circle over the tree house floor, whispering words that Jack couldn't understand, except for *Cozumel.* Slowly, magically, a small paperback book took shape on the floor.

Teddy picked up the book. "Your travel guide," he said proudly. "Cozumel and the Yucatán Peninsula."

He showed the book to Jack and Annie. The cover was a collage of several small paintings and photos. One showed a large, fancy hotel, another showed a stone pyramid, and a third showed a person snorkeling.

Teddy turned the book over and read from the back cover:

Visit Cozumel and the Yucatán Peninsula! Stay in a luxury spa hotel! See ancient Mayan pyramids and ruins! Snorkel in the clear blue water of the Caribbean Sea!

"Oh, wow! My dream vacation!" said Annie.

"I'll get our snorkeling gear!" said Jack.

"I'll grab our phone to take photos!" said Annie.

Jack and Annie hurried down the rope ladder. Annie took their cell phone from her handlebar bag and put it in one of the pockets of her tunic. Jack grabbed their swim bag, and they climbed up to Teddy.

"We're ready!" said Annie.

Teddy handed her the travel book. "Take this to guide you," he said. "And take this, too." He reached into his cloak and pulled out a green velvet coin purse. He handed the purse to Jack.

Jack opened the purse and took out three golden coins. "What are these?"

"We want you to have as much fun as possible on your holiday," said Teddy. "Each of these coins contains a bit of magic. Throw one into the air, make a wish, and your wish shall come true."

"Seriously? That's great!" said Annie.

"Yes," said Teddy. "You may wish for anything!

The only requirement is that the magic be used to help you have fun."

"This is going to be a great trip," said Jack. He put the purse with the magic coins into his bag.

"To Cozumel now you must go!" said Teddy.

"But, wait—are you sure we don't have a mission of some kind?" said Jack. They'd never been on a journey without an assignment from Morgan or Merlin.

"Yes, indeed, you do have a mission," said Teddy. "As I told you, your mission is to have a wonderful time."

"Nothing else?" said Jack.

"Nothing else," Teddy said with a smile.

"Wow," said Annie. "Can you come, too, and have a wonderful time at the beach with us?"

"I wish I could," said Teddy. "But I have to do more errands for Morgan and Merlin today— none quite as delightful as this one, however. You must tell me all about your journey when we meet again."

"Of course we will!" said Annie. "Come back to Frog Creek soon."

"I plan to," said Teddy. "Do you have all you need?"

"Yes!" said Jack. "And you don't need to magically change our clothes. We're already dressed for the beach."

"Excellent. Go now," said Teddy.

Annie pointed at the cover of the travel guide. "I wish we could go there," she said.

"To have a wonderful time," added Jack.

The wind started to blow.

The tree house started to spin.

It spun faster and faster.

Then everything was still.

Absolutely still.

CHAPTER TWO

Cozumel

Afternoon sunlight flooded into the tree house. Jack heard the sound of waves softly lapping the shore. He and Annie looked out the window. The tree house had landed in a palm tree overlooking snow-white sand and a turquoise-blue sea. Near the beach was the stone pyramid pictured on the cover of the travel guide.

"Cozumel," Jack said.

"Paradise," Annie said.

"Where is everyone?" said Jack, looking

around. There were no other tourists—no swimmers, surfers, or sunbathers. There were no sightseers. There were no vehicles parked near the Mayan pyramid.

"I don't know . . . ," Annie said. "I thought there'd be, you know, luxury spa hotels and fancy restaurants."

"It's weird," said Jack.

"Maybe it's just the perfect beach," said Annie, shrugging.

"Yeah, but . . ." Jack looked through their travel guide until he found a photo that seemed to match the deserted shoreline with the pyramid. "This looks like the same place." He read the caption:

On the southwest Caribbean coast is a nature preserve.

"Oh, cool! We landed in a nature preserve!" said Annie. "That's why it looks so natural."

"Right . . . ," said Jack. He read on:

Dazzling coral reefs are just a short distance offshore. Beginning snorkelers can
swim without losing sight of land.

"Yay!" said Annie. "We did come to the perfect
place—a nature preserve with a coral reef, just
like Randy and Jenny's."

"Yep!" said Jack. "Let's snorkel first. Then
maybe check out that pyramid. It looks cool."

"Good plan," said Annie. She started down the
rope ladder.

Jack put the travel guide into the swim bag
with their snorkel gear. He hung the bag on his
shoulder and followed Annie. He stepped off the
ladder and stood with her in the shade of the tree.

"Oh, man . . . ," said Jack, sighing.

A fresh, salty ocean breeze wafted over them.
White sand sparkled in the warm sunlight.

"This is a good view," said Annie. "I'll take a
picture. No, even better, a video." She reached
into the pocket of her tunic and pulled out their
cell phone. Pointing the phone at the beach, she

clicked the "record" button and spoke loudly: "Jack and I are in Cozumel, at a beautiful beach on a nature preserve, and this—"

"Hey, stop!" said Jack. "What if Mom and Dad see that? You have to erase it."

"Oh, you're right!" said Annie. She laughed as she deleted the video. "No big deal, Mom and Dad, we just took a little detour to Mexico on our way home from the lake." She put the phone in Jack's bag. "Okay! No camera on this trip."

"Let's hit the water," said Jack. As they started across the beach, their flip-flops sank into the fine, sugary sand. Seagulls cawed overhead.

"It's easier to go barefoot," said Annie. She and Jack stopped and put their flip-flops into Jack's bag.

"Hey, what's that?" Annie pointed to a raft lying on the sand.

"Whoa," said Jack. They hurried over to the raft. It was made of bamboo poles lashed together with leather strips. A paddle lay beside it. Jack looked around for its owner, but no one was in sight. "Who left it here?"

"It must belong to the nature preserve," said Annie. "I'll bet it's for tourists to use. Why else would it just be lying here? It's got a paddle and everything. Want to try it?"

"What? Put it in the water?" said Jack.

"Yes," said Annie. "It'll be fun! Say yes."

"No!" Jack said.

"Oh, Jack. Please! We can paddle out to the reef. Look how calm the water is! It'll be super-fun," said Annie.

Jack started to say no again, but he stopped. *It would actually be super-fun,* he thought. "Well, if we take it, we have to stay close to shore, and keep a lookout for its owner, just in case—"

"Okay, okay," said Annie. "I'll row!"

She grabbed the paddle, and Jack dragged the raft over the wet sand. He pushed it from the bubbling sea-foam into the cool, clear water.

"She floats!" said Annie.

Gentle waves lapped the sides of the raft. "Okay, you hop on first," said Jack. He put their bag on

the raft and then held it steady while Annie climbed onto the bamboo poles. The raft kept floating.

"Good, good . . . now me," said Jack as he climbed aboard.

The raft dipped a bit lower in the water, but it easily held them both.

"Yay! Now let's find the reef!" said Annie. "I'll take us there." As she began to paddle, the breeze helped push the raft over small ocean swells. "This is a great raft!"

"I'll bet the ancient Mayans made them just like this," said Jack.

"So who were the ancient Mayans exactly?" said Annie.

"I don't know a lot about them," said Jack. "But I know they had a huge civilization over a thousand years ago. They built pyramids and designed a special calendar."

"Well, they sure made good rafts," said Annie. As she pushed the paddle through the water, the raft moved farther out to sea.

"The breeze helped push the raft over small ocean swells."

About a hundred yards out, Jack held up his hand. "Okay, let's stop here," he said. "We don't want to get too far away from land. Let's look underwater for the reef. The book said it was near the shore."

"Right," said Annie. "You snorkel first. I'll stay with the raft."

"You sure?"

"Sure."

"Thanks." Jack reached into the swim bag. Before he pulled out their snorkel gear, he looked up *Cozumel, coral reefs* in the travel guide. He read aloud:

The coral reefs of Cozumel are visited by an average of 1,500 tourists a day. Coral—

"Really?" Annie interrupted. "I don't see one single tourist."

"I know. I don't understand that," said Jack. He kept reading:

Coral is made of animals, not plants. Since a coral reef is very delicate and takes a

very long time to grow, swimmers and snorkelers must avoid touching it or kicking it with their flippers.

"Makes sense," said Jack, closing the book. "Look. Don't touch. Just like at a museum."

"Got it," said Annie.

Jack put his glasses and the travel guide in the inside pocket of the swim bag. Then he unpacked all their swimming gear. While Annie held the raft steady with the paddle, Jack buckled on one of the life vests, squeezed his feet into flippers, and attached the snorkel to his face mask. Finally he pulled on the mask, covering his eyes and nose, and adjusted the strap. He inhaled through his nose, causing the mask to create a vacuum so water couldn't seep in.

"Balance me, so the raft doesn't flip over," Jack said to Annie.

Annie balanced the raft while Jack sat on the edge. As he slipped down into the sea, his life vest kept him from going under. Bobbing in the water, he placed the end of the snorkel tube into his mouth.

"Have fun!" Annie called.

Jack waved to her. Then he started swimming facedown along the surface of the water, gently kicking his flippers. Looking through his mask, he saw only a few fish at first. But then he saw more . . . and more . . . and *more*! Suddenly he couldn't believe his eyes.

CHAPTER THREE

Attack!

The underwater coral reef was huge, and the world around it was teeming with life. Seaweed waved in the gentle current. Pink and orange coral branched out in all directions. And *hundreds* of fish, as colorful as jelly beans, swam among the plants and the lacy coral.

Jack saw sleek, skinny fish, spiny fish, and flat fish. He saw fish that looked like butterflies, porcupines, and spindly stars.

As he kept swimming and looking through his mask, Jack saw green turtles feeding on algae.

"Jack saw sleek, skinny fish, spiny fish, and flat fish."

He saw huge crabs, jellyfish, and even a stingray among the wavy grasses.

But nothing Jack saw scared him, and none of the creatures seemed afraid of him, either. With his mask and flippers, Jack figured he looked like just another strange sea animal. A yellow-striped fish darted directly up to his mask, looked him in the eyes, then darted off again. A school of tiny white fish swam over his body, tickling him like feathers.

As he drifted around the reef, Jack saw orange starfish clustered over the coral ridges and tiny yellow sea horses bobbing near the coral branches. *Annie would love those little horses,* he thought.

Annie! Jack had been having such a great time, he'd forgotten all about Annie! Treading water, he pulled the snorkel out of his mouth, lifted his mask, and looked around for her. The raft was far away. The offshore breeze had pushed it farther out to sea. Jack waved and shouted, "Annie!"

Annie waved back. She paddled toward him.

"Your turn!" Jack said, gasping, when he reached the raft.

"How was it?" said Annie, pulling off her tunic.

"Unbelievable!" said Jack, climbing aboard. "You're going to love it!" He put his glasses back on and pulled off his flippers. "It's like a beautiful garden! Turtles! Starfish. And look for the tiny yellow sea horses around the coral!"

"I can't wait!" said Annie, cramming her feet into her flippers. "Here." She handed Jack the paddle. "You have to paddle pretty hard—the wind's pushing the raft."

"I noticed," said Jack. "Swim toward the beach, and you'll see the reef. I'll paddle after you. Then we'll head back to shore."

"Good plan!" Annie pulled on her mask and stuck the snorkel in her mouth. Jack balanced the raft as Annie sat on the edge.

"Have fun!" said Jack.

The raft rocked as Annie slid into the water. She started swimming back toward the reef.

Jack tried to follow close behind her, but the current kept pushing the raft farther out to sea. For a long time, he paddled hard just to stay in place. At one point, the current was so strong the raft turned sideways. Jack struggled to turn it back toward the beach.

When he got the raft under control again, he looked back toward the reef area. *He couldn't see Annie.* The waves had gotten higher. The sea seemed vast, and not nearly as safe and friendly.

Jack looked in every direction. Finally he saw something farther out to sea. *Can that be Annie's snorkel? Why would she swim so far out?* he wondered.

"Jack!"

He turned around.

Annie was bobbing on a wave not far from the raft. "It *is* incredible!" she shouted, holding up her mask. "Totally incredible!"

"Come on! Get aboard!" Jack yelled. "We have to go back! The current's too strong! Or maybe the wind! Whatever, we have to get back!"

Something else was bothering Jack—really bothering him. *What was that thing I saw?* he wondered. He turned and looked out to sea again.

Jack froze in horror. That *thing* was still sticking up out of the water. Now it was closer, and he could see what it was. It was a fin, a large fin. The fin was slicing swiftly through the water, heading straight for them.

"GET ON THE RAFT!" Jack screamed to Annie. "HURRY!" He began frantically paddling toward her, struggling against the current. When he looked over his shoulder, he saw the huge fin still zigzagging toward them.

"HURRY!" Jack shrieked.

Annie flung herself toward the raft. Grabbing the side, she gasped for air. "What's wrong?" she sputtered. "Why are you freaking out?"

"Just get on board!" he cried.

"Why?"

"Don't ask! Get on! Or *die!*" he yelled.

Annie clambered aboard. "What is it?" she asked, pulling off her mask and snorkel. "What did you see?"

"Look behind us!" Jack shouted. He was still struggling with the paddle, trying to point the raft toward shore.

"Ahhhh! Shark!" Annie cried. "Jack, a shark!"

"I *know!*" said Jack.

"Let's go! Go!" cried Annie.

"I'm trying!" said Jack. He looked over his shoulder. The shark fin moved toward them. Then it started to circle the raft.

Sharks circle their prey before they attack! Jack remembered. Using all his strength, he tried to turn the raft and head back to shore. But the wind and waves were too strong.

"Where is it?" cried Annie. "Where did it go?"

With the waves rising, Jack couldn't see the shark fin, either. "Maybe it's gone!" he said.

"AHHHH!" screamed Annie.

The shark's huge head came over the side of the raft, its mouth wide open.

"AHHHH!" yelled Jack. Without thinking, he raised his paddle and whacked the giant shark on the nose. The shark reared up and dug its jagged teeth into the wooden paddle, ripping it out of Jack's hand. Then the creature sank back down into the sea, and its fin glided away through the water.

"It's gone!" said Annie.

"*Not* gone!" cried Jack. "Look!"

The shark had moved away from the raft, but it was circling them again.

"We need magic, Jack!" shouted Annie. "We have to use a gold coin!"

"We can only use them to have fun!" said Jack.

"You don't think it would be fun to escape that shark?" said Annie. She pulled out the green velvet purse with the gold coins. She took out one of the three coins and held it up. The magic coin glittered in the Caribbean sunshine. "We wish to have fun escaping that shark!" she shouted. She tossed the coin high into the air. Like a tiny fireworks display, it burst into a shower of fiery red and blue sparks.

The raft suddenly spun like a top. Then it shot up the face of a large wave.

"The raft crested the wave, slid down the other side, and zoomed farther out to sea."

"AHHHH!" Jack and Annie screamed.

The raft crested the wave, slid down the other side, and zoomed farther out to sea. Another swell lifted the raft, then brought it down smoothly. And again, the raft shot across the surface of the water.

Jack and Annie held on to each other as the raft rolled over one swell after another, rising and dipping in rhythm with the waves. Sea spray blasted them. Salt water sloshed over the sides, but magically Jack and Annie stayed aboard.

"It's like the Bullet ride at Wade City Water Park!" Annie cried.

It is *like a water park ride,* Jack thought. But he was still in shock. *Where'd the shark go?* he wondered. *Are there other sharks? How will we get back without a paddle?*

"I love this!" shouted Annie, laughing. "It's so much fun!"

Finally the exhilaration of the ride overcame Jack's worries. As if harnessing the wind and current, the raft kept sliding up and down the swells, heading west. Seagulls followed it, shrieking overhead.

The raft kept roller-coastering across the sea, sliding up and down over more waves. Moving with great speed, the raft seemed to know exactly where to go.

"Hey, land! Is that land?" Annie said, pointing across the water.

Jack saw a jagged rocky coastline with a strip of gleaming white sand. "Yes! Yes!" he shouted. "It's land!"

CHAPTER FOUR

Where Are We?

The raft slowed down. As it floated toward the distant shore, the sea changed, becoming calm and smooth. The seagulls were silent.

"Where are we?" Annie asked.

"I'll check," said Jack. He reached into their waterproof bag and pulled out the travel guide. He quickly found a map inside. He pointed to the tip of Cozumel. Then he moved his finger across the Caribbean, landing on the eastern shore of the Yucatán Peninsula. Dotting the shoreline were symbols for hotels and resorts.

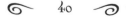

Jack showed the map to Annie. "I
come to the shore of the Yucatán Pe...
said.

"Cool," said Annie.

Jack read aloud from the guide:

> Vacationers flock to the eastern coast of
> the Yucatán of Mexico. Along the coast are
> comfortable luxury spa hotels and four-star
> Mexican restaurants. Tour buses visit Mayan
> ruins and hidden sinkholes filled with water.

"Hidden sinkholes filled with water?" said
Jack. "That sounds weird." He kept reading:

> Cruise ships dock at ports along the coast
> while ferries take tourists over the Caribbean
> to Cozumel.

"Good news," said Jack. "We can take a ferry
back to Cozumel. Then we won't have to worry
about sharks anymore." He looked around. "I

wonder why we haven't seen any ferries or cruise ships."

"Maybe they're docked in their ports now," said Annie. "It's late afternoon. It'll be dark soon." The sun was low in the sky. Soon it would sink behind the jagged cliff.

"Makes sense. I guess we'll have to catch the ferry first thing tomorrow," said Jack.

"Cool, we can stay in one of those comfortable luxury spa hotels the guide talks about," said Annie. "Doesn't that sound good?"

"Yeah, really good," said Jack. He was ready for a little comfort and luxury.

"And get dinner, too," said Annie, "like at a four-star Mexican restaurant."

"Great," said Jack. He loved Mexican food, and he was starving.

"We'd just be doing our mission," said Annie.

"Yep," said Jack. "Having a good time."

"Oh, look!" said Annie, pointing toward shore. "What's that? Up there!"

Jack saw stone buildings high on top of the cliff. "I'll bet those are Mayan ruins," he said, "like that pyramid we saw in Cozumel."

"Look it up," said Annie.

Jack flipped through their travel guide until he found a photo that looked like the same rocky cliff with the same stone buildings. "I found it," he said. He read aloud:

> **Yucatán Park is a tourist attraction on the east coast of the Yucatán. In ancient times it was a port city for Mayans sailing around the Caribbean. Today, it's a theme park that welcomes vacationers from all over the world.**

"A *theme* park!" said Annie. "What's the theme?"

Jack turned the page and saw Mayan dancers in tall feather headdresses. "I think the theme is ancient Mayan life."

"Oh, that's cool," said Annie.

Jack read more:

**Tourists flock to song-and-dance spectac-
ulars that take them through Mayan history.
A walking path connects the park to a hotel
zone.**

"Wow, song-and-dance spectaculars!" said Annie. "I'd love to see one of those!"

"I'd love to find a luxury hotel first," said Jack.

"Watch out!" said Annie. The raft was heading
for a pile of rocks at the edge of the water.

"Turn!" Jack shouted.

Amazingly, the raft swerved to the right and
missed the rocks. A wave then carried it into a
sheltered cove below the cliff. The raft slid over
bubbly foam at the edge of the sea and stopped on
pebbly wet sand.

Their magic ride had come to an end.

"Safe!" said Annie. "Our wish came true. We
had a fun ride."

"A lot of fun," said Jack. Even the terrifying shark attack didn't seem like such a big deal anymore, especially now that they could catch a ferry back to Cozumel in the morning.

As Jack and Annie packed up their gear, the sun was sinking behind the rocky bluff, turning the sky pink, then purple. Jack's face was warm with sunburn, but his body felt chilled in the sudden cool air. He was looking forward to settling into a nice hotel room.

"Okay!" he said. "Let's find that hotel zone."

"Let's check out the Mayan theme park first," said Annie.

"It must be closed by now," said Jack. "It's almost nighttime."

"Okay," said Annie, sighing. "But we have to visit it first thing tomorrow before we go back."

"Sure," said Jack. "I'd love to know more about Mayan history." He and Annie put on their flip-flops and stepped off the raft. "Uh-oh, I just thought of something."

"What?" said Annie.

"We need *money*," said Jack.

"Oh, right, for a hotel and dinner and the theme park," said Annie.

"And ferry tickets," said Jack.

Annie grinned. "No problem!" she said. "We use one of our gold coins to wish for money so we can have a good time."

Jack laughed. "Okay," he said. "That should work."

He reached in their bag, found the velvet purse, and took out a second gold coin. "We'll just have one left after we use this one."

"I know," said Annie. "But I think we can have lots of fun here even without magic."

"So how much should we wish for?" asked Jack.

"How about five hundred?" said Annie.

"*What?* Are you serious?" said Jack. "No kid carries around five hundred dollars."

"Well, then maybe we should wish for a credit card instead?" said Annie.

"Yeah, and how do you expect Morgan to pay a credit card bill?" said Jack.

"Okay. Back to five hundred dollars. We

need enough for the luxury spa hotel, a four-star dinner, breakfast, and tickets for the theme park and ferry."

"Okay, okay," said Jack. "Five hundred. I still think it's too much." He held up the coin. "Get ready for dollar bills to rain down on us."

"Ready," said Annie. She held out both hands.

"We wish for five hundred dollars—to have a good time!" said Jack. He tossed the gold coin into the air. Again, like tiny fireworks, it burst into a shower of fiery red and blue sparks. When the sparks cleared, nothing rained down from the air.

"Oh, no," said Jack. "It didn't work."

"Yes it did! Look!" said Annie. Sitting in the middle of the raft was a neat stack of crisp green bills. She picked them up and counted. "Hurray! We have ten fifty-dollar bills."

"Great!" said Jack. "We can probably change them into Mexican money—pesos—when we get to the hotel."

"No problem," said Annie. "Give me the purse. We'll put the money in with our last gold coin."

Jack handed Annie the purse, and she stuffed the wad of bills inside.

"Before we go, we should pull the raft higher up on the sand so it doesn't wash out to sea," said Jack. "Maybe someone else can use it—if they can find a paddle."

Jack and Annie leaned over and gripped the raft.

"Heave ho!" said Annie. And together they pulled it higher up on the beach.

"Wait. Hear that?" said Annie. "Listen! It's coming from up there!"

The sounds of musical instruments were coming from the top of the cliff. "The theme park *is* open!" said Annie. "Maybe they're doing one of those song-and-dance spectaculars we read about! Let's go see!"

"I'd rather just get to a hotel," said Jack. "We've had a full day."

"Oh, please," begged Annie. "Let's check out the show really fast, and then we'll go straight to the hotel, I promise."

Jack listened to the music for a moment. It was filled with the haunting sound of flutes and thumping drums. It sounded mysterious and joyful. "Okay," he said.

"Come on!" Annie started across the sand.

Jack grabbed their bag. "How do we get up the cliff?" he said, hurrying after her.

"I saw some steps when we were coming in!" said Annie. "They're just around those rocks!"

As Jack followed Annie around a pile of boulders, a cool wind blew across the sand. The full moon had turned the sea to silver.

CHAPTER FIVE

Yucatán Theme Park

"There! Those are the steps I was talking about," said Annie. She pointed to a rickety wooden stairway clinging to the side of the cliff.

"*That?*" said Jack.

"I know, it doesn't look safe," said Annie. "But I don't see any other way to get up there."

Jack looked up and down the beach. "Me neither. I guess we'll have to try it."

Lugging their bag, Jack followed Annie to the stairs. Annie started up first, the weathered boards creaking with her weight.

"Careful," said Jack. "Hold on to the railing."

"You too!" Annie called down.

Jack started climbing the rickety stairway. Gripping the handrail, he took one step at a time as the wind shook the stairs, and the sound of drums and flutes floated down from above.

Suddenly Jack's foot broke through one of the boards! Hanging on tightly to the railing, he leapt to the next step as the broken one crashed to the ground.

"You okay?" said Annie.

"Yeah, barely," Jack answered.

As he kept climbing, he clung to the railing and gingerly placed one foot after the other. Finally he followed Annie from the top step onto the rocky ground at the top of the cliff.

"We made it!" Annie said.

"I can't believe they built such a bad staircase!" said Jack.

"They probably want it to look as real as possible," said Annie, "like in olden times."

"Yeah, but how about *safe*?" said Jack. "If

someone falls—or this whole thing comes crashing down—people could really get hurt."

"We should tell our hotel to post a warning or something," said Annie.

"Yeah. *Avoid the rickety staircase with the broken step,*" said Jack.

As he caught his breath, he listened to the drum and flute music coming from behind a high stone wall. The smell of wood smoke filled the air. By now the full moon had risen over the park, giving everything a bluish tint.

"It sounds great, doesn't it?" said Annie.

"Yeah, it does," said Jack. He had to admit that the theme park show seemed really inviting.

"I wonder how we get inside," said Annie.

"Hold on," said Jack. He took out their travel guide. By the light of the moon, he studied the map. "It looks like a wall runs all the way around the park. And the entrance is on the other side, with a ticket booth. . . . Oh, and there's a visitors bureau! They can help us find a hotel."

"But we're checking out the show *first*, right?" Annie said.

"Sure, let's go," said Jack.

As they started along the wall, bellowing horn sounds came from inside the park. "Whoa, what's that?" said Annie. She ran ahead.

When Jack caught up with her, she was looking through a narrow opening in the wall. "It's *definitely* a song-and-dance spectacular," she said. "Look at the great costumes!"

Annie stepped aside so Jack could peek through the opening. He saw the long shadows of stone buildings. In front of the buildings was an open square, bright with firelight. Dancers and musicians were performing around a roaring bonfire. Dozens of people watched from the sides, some standing and some sitting on the ground.

"It looks great," said Jack. "Let's find the entrance."

"Oh, let's just sneak in through here," said Annie, "before the show ends."

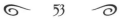

"What about our tickets?" said Jack.

"If we spend time looking for the ticket booth, we'll miss the show!" said Annie. "We can pay on the way out. This is a chance of a lifetime."

"Okay," said Jack.

"Yes!" said Annie. She turned sideways and slid through the narrow opening. "See? No problem," she said from the other side.

"Take this," said Jack. He pushed their bulky bag through the opening. Then he squeezed sideways between the thick slabs of rock.

Jack took his bag back from Annie, and they hurried across the grounds of the park. When they got close to the bonfire, they stood near the back of the square.

The male dancers had feathered headdresses and beautiful feathered cloaks. They wore arm and leg bracelets made of gold and silver. They had painted faces and tattoos. Some of them waved spears and shields as they shook their bodies.

Near the dancers, several musicians played wooden flutes. Others rattled hollow gourd instruments and rang loud bells. Some clapped sticks together, while still others banged huge turtle-shell drums and blew on giant conch shells that made deep bellowing sounds.

While the dancers danced and the musicians played, actors moved about in front of the crowd, miming a story. They wore jaguar masks, crocodile masks, and bird masks. They bowed to two regal-looking men who sat on thronelike wooden seats on a platform. The two men wore enormous head-dresses and animal-skin capes. Behind them stood a row of feathered warriors.

"I'll bet those two guys are supposed to be ancient Mayan kings," whispered Annie, "and the ones behind them must be their bodyguards. This *is* spectacular!"

Jack had to agree, even though none of it made sense to him. He looked around at the crowd watching the show. He noticed that the women and girls wore colorful dresses and large pieces of jewelry. The men and boys wore loincloths or feathered robes. Many men wore headdresses.

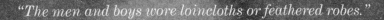
"The men and boys wore loincloths or feathered robes."

"Don't you think it's a little weird that everyone in the audience is wearing a costume?" Jack whispered.

"I love it," said Annie. "Maybe this show is like a reality show, where even the audience plays a part. I'll bet when you buy a ticket, you get a costume. I'll find out." She stepped over to some young boys in feathered robes who were watching the dancers. "Excuse me," she said.

A couple of boys turned around and looked at her. They jumped back as if frightened. Before Annie could ask about their costumes, one of them darted to a woman, grabbed her hand, and pointed to Annie. The woman cried out in alarm.

"Whoa, what's that about?" said Jack.

"I think they're just acting," Annie said.

More and more people were turning to look at Jack and Annie. Some whispered and pointed. All had expressions of fear and wonder.

"I don't think these people are acting," said Jack.

"Really?" said Annie.

"Yeah, this feels really weird."

The music stopped. The musicians put down their instruments and stared with the rest of the crowd. Several men with spears started toward Jack and Annie.

"Let's go!" said Jack.

"Wait," said Annie. "It's part of the show! Don't you want to play a role in it?"

"No! Let's go!" said Jack. He grabbed Annie's hand and pulled her along, heading back the way they'd come. As he hurried toward the wall, he heard shouting behind them.

When they reached the narrow opening, Jack looked over his shoulder. The feathered men with spears were coming right at them. A few curious children were following the spear carriers.

Jack frantically tried to push the bag through the opening ahead of him, but it got stuck. He shoved as hard as he could, but the bag didn't budge.

"Don't you want to find out what's going on?" said Annie.

"No! I just want to get away from this crazy show!" said Jack. "I don't want to perform in it!"

"Too late!" said Annie.

Jack looked back. The feathered warriors had nearly reached them. Jack pulled hard on the bag, yanking with such force that he fell backward, and the bag landed on top of him. A moment later, spear carriers were standing over him. Several surrounded Annie, too.

"Hi!" said Annie. "This is all part of the song-and-dance spectacular, right?"

None of the men answered.

"We didn't know where to get tickets," she said. "We, uh, we thought maybe we could pay on the way out?"

Again, no one answered. Instead the spear carriers turned to one another and spoke in frantic whispers. "Who are they?" "What are they?" "Where do they come from?"

A girl about Annie's age stepped forward. Like Annie, she had long, thick braids and bangs, but her hair was shiny black. The girl stared at Annie curiously and then smiled a big smile.

"Why did they stop the show?" Annie asked the girl. "What's going on?"

The girl kept staring at Annie. "Who are you?" she asked. Before Annie could answer, a woman rushed forward, grabbed the girl, and pulled her away.

One of the warriors pointed his spear at Jack. "Come," he said. "To the House of Columns."

"Um . . . actually, we'd rather go to the hotel zone," Jack said.

The man stared at him.

"But whatever's closest," said Jack. "We're not picky."

The warrior gently prodded Jack with the tip of his spear. "Go," he said.

Without another word, Jack and Annie began marching across the grounds. *If this is all part of the show,* Jack thought, *these guys are taking it way too seriously.*

Followed by the spear carriers, Jack and Annie walked through the blue moonlight, until they came to a stone building with columns. The head warrior ushered them up uneven steps, opened a heavy wooden door, and motioned for them to enter.

"Wait for the king," the warrior said.

The cold, empty room had only a single window, which let in a shaft of moonlight. The warrior closed the heavy door, leaving Jack and Annie alone in the House of Columns.

CHAPTER SIX

Heart-of-the-Wind

"Well, I wouldn't exactly call this a luxury hotel," said Annie. She shivered. A damp wind was blowing through the open window.

Jack was too stunned to speak. He reached into the swim bag and pulled out the travel guide. He walked to the window and studied the cover by moonlight. "Oh . . . ," he whispered, and then pointed to one of the small paintings. "I think I get it now."

"Get what?" said Annie.

Jack looked at her. "This isn't a theme park."

"I was starting to think that, too," said Annie. "But what is it?"

"It's *real*," said Jack.

"Real?" said Annie. "What do you mean, *real*?"

"I think we've accidentally come to the actual time of ancient Mayans," said Jack.

"Like when?" said Annie.

"Like maybe over a thousand years ago, when they wore feathers and fought with spears."

"But—how is that possible?" said Annie. "Teddy sent us to Cozumel *now*, in *our* time!"

"That's what he was *supposed* to do," said Jack. "But maybe when you pointed at the cover of the book, you pointed at the painting of the ancient pyramid the way it looked, like, over a thousand years ago. Teddy must not have known the pyramid painting would send us back to Cozumel *then* instead of *now*."

"Oh. Wow. You mean all this time we've been in an ancient world?" said Annie.

"Yep. We didn't land in a modern nature preserve," said Jack.

"Oh," said Annie.

"That's why we didn't see any tourists or ferries or cruise ships," said Jack.

"Right," said Annie, nodding. She looked back at the cover of the guide. "Too bad I didn't point to the luxury hotel."

"No kidding," said Jack.

"These guys have probably never seen people like us before," said Annie.

"Probably?" said Jack. "Definitely. We're from the future—more than a thousand years in the future."

"What should we do?" said Annie.

"There's only one thing to do—we have to get out of here and back to the tree house," said Jack. "Before the king comes."

"Can we escape through the window?" Annie walked over and looked out the open window. "Darn. Guards are patrolling the building."

"So we can't get out that way," said Jack.

"Oh, I know what we can do!" said Annie. "We can use our last gold coin to help us!"

"Of course! Perfect!" said Jack. He grabbed their swim bag. "Yes, yes, yes. We'll make a wish to escape all the way back to the tree house! With no warriors capturing us or sharks attacking us! I think that would qualify as fun."

"Let's make a wish to fly from this window, across the sea!" said Annie. "That would be *so* fun!"

"No kidding!" said Jack. He knelt on the floor and dug inside the bag for the velvet coin purse. "Where is it?" He pulled everything out: flippers, life vests, snorkels, and face masks. "Where is it? Where's that coin purse?"

Jack turned the bag upside down and shook it. He and Annie shook the flippers and life vests, too, but no small green velvet purse fell out.

"It's not here," said Jack. "Did you put it back in here?"

Annie looked confused. "Did I?"

"That's what I'm asking," said Jack. "Did you?"

"I don't know," said Annie. "I remember I put the five hundred dollars in the purse . . . and then

we pushed the raft . . . and then we heard the music and—"

"So when did you put the purse back in the bag?" asked Jack.

"I—I don't know," said Annie. "Maybe I didn't. . . . Maybe I put it down on the sand . . . to push the raft. . . ."

"Seriously?" said Jack.

"That's what I sort of remember now that I think about it . . . ," whispered Annie. "Oh, no! I lost all our money and the magic coin! I'm so sorry!"

"It's okay," said Jack. "It'll be okay. We just need to get out of here and climb back down to the beach before the king comes."

"And find our coin purse!" said Annie.

"Right," said Jack. He took a deep breath. "Okay, one thing at a time. First, let's—" Before he could say more, the door swung open. Jack quickly crammed everything back into their bag.

The room was suddenly filled with fiery light.

Warriors with burning torches entered the room.

Several women followed the warriors. The women had large jade ornaments in their ears and wore dresses woven with red, yellow, and purple threads. They placed flowers on the floor, along with bowls filled with corn, beans, chili peppers, and pineapple slices.

Two men then stepped into the room—the same two who had sat on the thrones. *They must be kings,* Jack thought. *But why are there two of them?* The two kings wore feather headdresses that were at least three feet high. Around their shoulders were jaguar skins. Their arms were covered with bracelets. The older-looking one had long white hair. A girl with black braids stood beside him—the same girl who'd spoken to Annie near the wall.

Everyone stared at Jack and Annie.

"Hi," said Annie.

"We come in peace," said Jack.

The younger of the two kings stepped forward.

"Who *are* you?" the man asked.

"Jack and Annie of Frog Creek, Pennsylvania," said Annie.

"How did you get here?" the king asked.

"By raft," said Jack, "from Cozumel."

The older king picked up the travel guide from the floor. "What is this?"

Oh, no! thought Jack. He'd forgotten to put their book back in the bag! The king turned the book upside down and sideways. He stared at the back and the front.

"It's a travel guide," Annie said helpfully.

"A travel guide?" the older man repeated. His face was lined with wrinkles, and his eyes were bright and alert. He opened the book and stared at a page. Pointing to a photo of a plane landing at the Cozumel airport, he looked puzzled.

"That's a plane," said Jack.

"It flies," said Annie. She moved her hand through the air. "Like a bird."

The older king looked at the younger king and shrugged. He ruffled the pages, and the book fell open to a photo of a cruise ship.

"He opened the book and stared at a page."

"That's an ocean liner," said Jack.

"It carries *thousands* of people across the ocean," said Annie.

The king turned to more photos: one showed a water-skier, and another showed an underwater tourist boat.

"Speedboat," said Annie. "Submarine."

The king turned the page and stared at a photo of skyscraper hotels. On the opposite page was a photo of a guest room with a girl working on a computer and a boy watching a football game on TV.

Neither Annie nor Jack tried to explain.

As the king turned more pages in the book, Jack glanced around the room. He caught the gaze of the young girl. She was the only person smiling.

Finally the old king closed the book and looked at Jack and Annie for a long time. He handed the book to Jack. Then he turned and nodded to the younger ruler. The two kings and the girl walked out the door back into the night. The women followed, and then the warriors.

One of the warriors left his flaming torch in

a stone sconce. Then he closed the door, leaving Jack and Annie alone again in the dimly lit room.

"I wonder what they were thinking," said Annie. "Are we their prisoners or their guests?"

"I don't know," said Jack, shaking his head. This dream vacation had turned into a nightmare.

"Should we eat the food?" asked Annie.

"I'm not hungry anymore," said Jack.

"Me neither," said Annie. "I just thought it might be polite."

"I guess we'd better learn more about ancient Mayans," Jack said. He opened the guide and found a section titled *Mayans*. By the light of the torch, he read aloud:

Today many Mayans live in Mexico and other parts of Central America. Long ago, before Columbus discovered the "New World," Mayans had their own civilization. They created their own calendar and a special form of picture writing. They were skilled farmers, astronomers, and architects.

Before Jack could read more, the door opened again. The girl with the bangs and shiny black braids slipped into the room. She closed the door and smiled at Jack and Annie.

"Hi," said Annie. "What's your name?"

"Heart-of-the-Wind," said the girl.

"That's a beautiful name," said Annie.

"Thank you," said Heart-of-the-Wind. "My father meets with his council now."

"Who's your father?" asked Annie.

"My father is the Great Sun," said the girl. "He rules the kingdom of Palenque. It is many days from here, in the jungle."

"Was the Great Sun the one who looked at our book?" asked Jack.

"Yes," said Heart-of-the-Wind. "He has been traveling the land to find his true heir. Weeks ago, we stopped here, in the City of Dawn, to visit with the king and rest. My father did not know that *this* would be the place where he would find what he was looking for." She smiled at Jack. "Do you understand?"

"Um . . . I'm not sure," said Jack. *What am I supposed to understand?* he thought.

"My father believes that *you* are the one he has been searching for," said Heart-of-the-Wind.

"Me?" said Jack.

"My father just told me that he believes the gods have sent you to be our next king," said Heart-of-the-Wind.

"Jack?" said Annie. "Your next king?"

"Jack," the girl said, nodding. "I am my father's only child. He has no sons. So he has decided to take Jack back to our kingdom and prepare him to be our ruler."

"Me?" Jack said again.

"Yes," said Heart-of-the-Wind. *"You* will be the next Great Sun of Palenque."

CHAPTER SEVEN

The Forest-of-Walking-Trees

Annie gasped, then burst out laughing.

Heart-of-the-Wind laughed, too. "Yes, it is wonderful news! I am glad it makes you happy," she said. "When the sun rises tomorrow, we will leave the City of Dawn and start the long journey back to Palenque. It will take us many moons to get there."

"But—but why *me*?" asked Jack.

"My father believes you are the answer to his prayers," said Heart-of-the-Wind. "He can see you have many things to teach our people."

"No, no I don't," said Jack. His words spilled over each other. "I don't know how to farm, I'm not an astronomer or a pyramid builder, I don't know anything about your Mayan calendar—" He stopped to catch his breath.

"My father will teach you these things," said Heart-of-the-Wind. "And you will teach us about the wonders in your—what did you call it?"

"Travel guide," said Annie.

"Yes," said Heart-of-the-Wind, "the wonders in your travel guide."

"No, I can't," said Jack. "I don't know how to make any of those things myself, like planes, submarines, skyscrapers, or computers. We live in a world with lots and lots of things, but we have to go to school and study for many years to understand how they work."

"Besides, my brother and I really need to go back to our own parents in Frog Creek, Pennsylvania," said Annie.

Heart-of-the-Wind looked confused. "Would your mother and father not think it a wonderful honor for Jack to be the next Great Sun of Palenque?"

"They might," said Annie, "but they would miss us too much if we came to live with you."

"That's right," said Jack. "We do lots of things with our parents. We have dinner and play games and read books."

"And talk and laugh," said Annie.

Heart-of-the-Wind lowered her head. "I have lost my own mother," she said. "We talked and laughed together, too. I miss her very much."

"So you understand?" Annie said softly. "We would miss our parents terribly. And it would break their hearts if we left them alone. We *have* to go back home."

The Mayan girl looked at Jack and Annie for a long moment. Then she nodded. "Yes. You must go back to your true mother and father," she said. "But I fear my father will not understand."

"So could you help us get back to the cove on the beach?" asked Jack. "So we can cross the sea back to Cozumel? And then go home?"

78

"To our mother and father," said Annie.

Heart-of-the-Wind took a deep breath. "Yes, I will help you. I will take you to the shore," she said. "Even though it will make my father sad."

"Thank you!" said Jack.

"At this time, there are watchmen on the wall," said the Mayan girl. "But I have discovered a hidden way to get to the sea. In the weeks we have stayed here, I have often slipped away at night to explore the forests or swim in the waves."

"Wow, you're brave," said Annie.

"I like the freedom of the dark," the Mayan girl said. "I can lead you wherever you want to go."

"That's great!" Jack said.

"There are still guards outside the door," said Heart-of-the-Wind. "I will hold their attention while you climb out the window. Wait for me at the wall where we first met."

"Got it," said Annie.

"Stay in the shadows," the Mayan girl said. "Be as quiet as cats." Then she slipped out the door, closing it behind her.

"Let's go!" said Annie.

"Wait," said Jack. "Let's take off our shoes. They make too much noise."

Jack and Annie pulled off their flip-flops and stuffed them in the bag. Barefoot, they stepped to the window. Annie climbed out first. "Take this," Jack whispered. He dropped the bag into Annie's waiting arms. Then he jumped silently to the ground. He could hear voices coming from the other side of the stone building: Heart-of-the-Wind and the guards.

Jack and Annie crept away from the House of Columns, moving through the shadows. The night was eerily still, as if everyone in the City of Dawn had disappeared until sunrise.

When they reached the break in the stone wall, they crouched down and waited for Heart-of-the-Wind. Jack saw the silhouettes of the guards standing on top of the wall. He counted four watchmen with bows and arrows facing the sea.

The Mayan girl suddenly appeared before them. Jack hadn't seen or heard her approach.

"Follow me," she whispered, and she led the way through the narrow opening in the wall.

Once they had all squeezed through, Heart-of-the-Wind surprised Jack by turning away from the sea and heading down through thick vegetation growing on the northern slope of the bluff. Jack and Annie followed her down the hill. Prickly bushes and shrubs scratched Jack's bare legs and feet, but he didn't stop. He wanted to be as fleet as Heart-of-the-Wind.

At the bottom of the hill, the Mayan girl waited for Jack and Annie to catch up. "To return to the beach, we must first travel through the Forest-of-Walking-Trees," she said.

"Forest-of-Walking-Trees?" said Annie. "That sounds cool. But sort of scary."

"Do not be afraid," said Heart-of-the-Wind. "They are very kind trees."

Jack laughed. "I like kind trees," he said.

"Me too," said Annie.

Heart-of-the-Wind led Jack and Annie to a moonlit swamp. As they sloshed through shallow water, Jack heard the hum of insects and the rustling of night creatures. The air smelled of salt water and rotting wood.

"Whoa, those trees *do* have legs!" said Annie, peering into the shadows.

"Those are just roots," said Jack. He'd seen pictures of tropical mangrove trees with their roots rising aboveground.

"No, those trees have legs," said Heart-of-the-Wind. "But they walk only at night. Hello!" she called in a whisper. "May we pass by?"

The wind blew, and the trees waved their branches. Their leaves rustled, whispering, *Yes, yes, yes.*

"Come," said the girl.

Jack and Annie followed Heart-of-the-Wind deeper into the watery forest, careful not to trip over roots and bushes. Jack jumped when something prickly darted between his ankles. He shuddered when something with lots of tiny legs ran down his arm. But he tried not to make a sound. He wanted to be like Heart-of-the-Wind. Nothing seemed to bother her as she moved silently and smoothly through the swamp.

Suddenly a raucous howling ripped through the darkness.

"Yikes!" said Annie.

Heart-of-the-Wind laughed. "It is only the Ones-Who-Tell-the-History-of-the-Forest," she said.

"Cool," said Jack. He knew the sounds came from howler monkeys, the loudest monkeys in the world. He'd learned about them on a nature show, but he preferred the Mayan girl's name for them. *Maybe in their language, the monkeys really are telling the history of the forest,* he thought.

"Come along," said Heart-of-the-Wind. As they started through the darkness again, a different sound came from nearby—a deep, ominous growl.

"Whoa!" whispered Jack.

Heart-of-the-Wind held up her hand. "Silence," she said, keeping her voice low. "He is watching us."

"Who?" whispered Annie.

"Jack and Annie followed Heart-of-the-Wind deeper into the watery forest, careful not to trip over roots and bushes."

"He-Who-Kills-with-One-Leap," the girl said.

"Oh, just him," whispered Jack, trying to make a joke.

Heart-of-the-Wind laughed softly. "Yes. Him. There," she said, pointing.

In the moonlight, Jack could see yellow eyes and spotted fur. *A jaguar!* he thought. "Um . . . should we go another way? Maybe?" he said.

"No. I will send him peaceful thoughts," said Heart-of-the-Wind.

"Good idea," whispered Annie.

She and Jack were silent as the Mayan girl stared for a long moment at the jaguar. Then she took a deep breath. "He says we may pass his way."

"He does?" said Jack.

"Cool," said Annie.

Heart-of-the-Wind led them past the tree where the jaguar crouched on a limb. Clutching his bag, Jack barely breathed as he slipped past the huge cat.

"Good night!" Heart-of-the-Wind called back to the jaguar.

"Thank you!" called Annie.

The cat growled again.

"He said, *Sure, no problem,*" said Jack.

Heart-of-the-Wind laughed at his joke, and Jack laughed, too. Despite the danger, he was having a good time.

Jack and Annie followed Heart-of-the-Wind as she forged on through the forest, climbing over tangles of roots and wading through knee-high water.

"She's like an Eagle Scout," Annie said to Jack.

"I was thinking more like a Navy SEAL," said Jack.

The Mayan girl came to a halt. "Do not go near that log," she whispered, pointing to a fallen tree trunk.

"Why not?" asked Jack.

"It lives," she said.

"It lives?" said Jack.

Heart-of-the-Wind broke off a twig and tossed it at the log. The log moved. It was the snout of a crocodile! Its huge mouth opened and closed.

Jack and Annie jumped back. They laughed at themselves and then followed Heart-of-the-Wind as she led them away from the crocodile. "He is called Earth-Monster-of-the-Underworld," she said.

"Good name," said Annie.

"To get to the sea, we must travel through the Underworld," said Heart-of-the-Wind.

"Um . . . and what's that exactly?" asked Jack.

"The home of the ancestor spirits," said the girl. "My father's warriors will not enter the Underworld. They are frightened by what they cannot see. But *I* am not afraid."

"Me neither," said Annie.

"Nope. Not one bit," said Jack, and he meant it. As long as they were with Heart-of-the-Wind, scary stuff didn't seem all that scary. At that moment, he wasn't afraid of anything.

CHAPTER EIGHT

Through the Underworld

"Soon we will enter the Underworld," said Heart-of-the-Wind. She led Jack and Annie through the mangrove forest until they came to a river hidden by trees and vines. As the leafy branches swayed in the breeze, moonlight danced on the silvery water.

"This is the Sacred Well," the Mayan girl said. "Our journey to the Underworld begins here." She stepped over to a hollowed-out log canoe at the water's edge. She picked up a wooden paddle lying beside the boat.

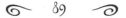

As Heart-of-the-Wind pushed the canoe into the Sacred Well, Jack turned to Annie. "Remember how the travel guide mentioned *sinkholes filled with water*?" he whispered. "This must be one of them."

"*Sacred Well* sounds way better than *sinkhole*, doesn't it?" whispered Annie.

"Definitely," said Jack.

Heart-of-the-Wind slipped down into the dugout canoe and picked up the paddle. "Please, climb in," she said.

Jack and Annie carefully lowered themselves down into the rough interior of the boat. Jack held their bag on his lap.

Heart-of-the-Wind began paddling through the waters of the Sacred Well. As she shifted her paddle from side to side, the log canoe glided over the shimmering river. It curved down a shadowy passageway between rocks and then arrived at the yawning mouth of a cave.

"*Now* we enter the Underworld," said Heart-of-the-Wind.

Moonlight shimmered on the underground river as the canoe glided in and out of light-filled passageways and tunnels. Water dripped and trickled down the cave walls. Soon one of the tunnels opened into a huge chamber that had a giant hole in the ceiling, letting in the full light of the moon.

"Oh, man," breathed Jack.

Huge columns of white rock stretched down from the ceiling of the cavern. The columns looked as if they were made of gleaming ice, and thousands of tiny icicle-like strands covered the craggy walls.

"What are those?" Annie asked.

"Stone sculptures made by the Rain God," said Heart-of-the-Wind.

Jack knew from a geology book that the formations were called stalactites. They were made by centuries of dripping and trickling water in caves. But he liked Heart-of-the-Wind's answer better.

The Mayan girl carefully steered the canoe around the gleaming columns. "Look there," she whispered. She pointed to a ledge in the chamber.

On the ledge was a platform that held carved wooden statues. Some looked like snarling jaguars, others like coiled serpents. The largest was a statue of an angry king with a terrible scowl. "They guard the Underworld and protect the ancestor spirits," Heart-of-the-Wind explained.

"Cool," said Annie.

Heart-of-the-Wind steered the canoe around a corner and into another cave tunnel. This tunnel was completely dark, without a trace of light. The air was cold and clammy. The canoe bumped against the rock walls. Jack reached out and felt the slippery, drippy stone. He pulled his hand back and shuddered.

As Heart-of-the-Wind paddled on through the black tunnel, Jack clutched his bag and tried to still his racing heart. The Underworld frightened him a little now: the tireless *drip-drip* of water, the strange statues of serpents and jaguars, and now the dank utter darkness of the tunnel.

"Where are the ancestor spirits?" whispered Annie.

"They are all around us," Heart-of-the-Wind whispered back. "They are watching everything we do."

Oh, man, Jack thought. No wonder the king's warriors were afraid to enter the Underworld.

"Do not be afraid," said the Mayan girl, as if she had read his thoughts. "I will protect you."

"Thank you," whispered Annie, sounding a little nervous herself.

Heart-of-the-Wind paddled through the twists and turns of the Underworld, until finally the canoe emerged onto a glistening pool that was open to the moonlit sky.

"Whew. We made it," said Annie.

"And lived to tell about it!" Jack said, only half joking.

"That was great," said Annie.

"You are both more brave than my father's men," said Heart-of-the-Wind.

"Finally the canoe emerged onto a glistening pool that was open to the moonlit sky."

"Not really," said Jack. But he secretly liked thinking of himself as being braver than an ancient Mayan warrior. "That was an incredible ride."

Heart-of-the-Wind paddled the canoe to the edge of the water. "We have arrived," she said.

Jack could hear ocean waves and the cries of gulls. The moon was going down. In the east, the sky was growing lighter.

Heart-of-the-Wind held the canoe steady as Jack and Annie climbed out onto the beach. The Mayan girl followed behind them, and Jack and Annie helped her pull the log canoe out of the pool, onto the cool sand. "The light of the dawn will be bright very soon," said Heart-of-the-Wind. "What will you do now?"

"We need to find something we lost," Annie said. "It's next to a raft we left on the beach."

"At least we hope it is," said Jack.

"Where is the raft?" the girl asked.

"In the cove below the City of Dawn," said Annie.

"Follow me," said Heart-of-the-Wind. "I will take you there."

 96

Checkout Receipt

Willits Branch Library
10/26/23 05:51PM
****

Borrower Number: 244334

Shadow of the shark /
36363001760396   Due: 11/16/23

TOTAL: 1

For account information, review items
being held, renew items, & more:
www.mendolibrary.org
TELECIRC (707) 340-5197

The Mayan girl led Jack and Annie down the misty beach. When they came to a pile of stones jutting into the sea, she stopped. "Stay close to the rocks so the watchmen cannot see us," she said. "They will not leave their post until the sun rises."

With the mist hiding them, Heart-of-the-Wind led Jack and Annie over the rocks. Jack could hear the waves breaking against the shore.

"And what will *you* do next?" Annie asked as they followed Heart-of-the-Wind. "Where will you go after we leave you?"

"I will return to my father," said the girl. "I will tell him that you have gone home to your own true father and mother."

"Will your father be mad?" asked Jack.

"Perhaps," said Heart-of-the-Wind. "He believed you were the answer to a question he has been asking for a long time: who will lead our people after he dies?"

"Okay. But *I* have a question for *him*," said Annie.

"What is your question?" said Heart-of-the-Wind. She stopped and looked back at Annie.

"I would like to ask him, 'Why can't your daughter, Heart-of-the-Wind, lead your people after you are gone?'" said Annie.

The Mayan girl laughed the biggest laugh she'd laughed all night. "You are crazy," she said.

"Seriously! That's a great question," said Jack. "Why can't *you* be the next Great Sun of Palenque?"

"Yes!" said Annie. "Where we come from, women are leaders of many countries and cities and states."

Heart-of-the-Wind looked shocked. "Truly? But that is not possible here. A female is not allowed to rule the Mayan people. Now you must hurry. Before the sun rises." She moved away from them, climbing over the rocks again, as if the matter were closed.

Jack and Annie hurried to keep up with Heart-of-the-Wind. Finally the three of them climbed over a big boulder and dropped down onto the sandy beach of the cove.

"Listen to me, Heart-of-the-Wind," said Annie. "You're as brave as any warrior—braver, really. You don't seem at all afraid of the forest or the Underworld."

"Right, and you know tons more than I do," said Jack. "You know your people. I'll bet you know a lot about farming, and you know how to use the Mayan calendar, right?"

Heart-of-the-Wind nodded. "Yes."

"*And* you know how to talk to jaguars," said Annie.

"And you're not afraid of the Rain God or the ancestor spirits," said Jack.

"So why can't you be a leader?" asked Annie.

Heart-of-the-Wind turned to look at the sea and slowly shook her head. "No, no, no . . . it is not possible . . . never."

"Okay. But just answer one question for me," said Annie. "Would you *like* to be the Great Sun of Palenque someday? If you *could* be, would you? Tell the truth."

Heart-of-the-Wind looked back at Annie and Jack. She smiled. "Yes. I would like to be the leader of my people."

"We know you would take good care of them!" said Annie. "Just like you've taken good care of us!"

"I would be fair and just," said Heart-of-the-Wind. "I would teach everyone to read our calendar and learn our writing. I would make certain that all of my people had enough fish, beans, and grains to eat."

"Heart-of-the-Wind, you must tell that to your father!" said Annie.

"He would laugh at me," said Heart-of-the-Wind. "He would never allow a girl to inherit his throne, not even a daughter he loves greatly. That would be against all the customs and traditions of our ancestors."

"Isn't there any way you could change his mind?" said Jack.

"Only a miracle could change the mind of my father about this," said Heart-of-the-Wind.

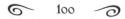

"Okay," said Annie. "I have an idea. What if _Jack_ told him?"

_"Me?"_ Jack said to Annie.

"Yes!" said Annie. "Heart-of-the-Wind, your father believes Jack came from a faraway place to teach new things to your people. So maybe Jack could teach him that girls can grow up to be great leaders, just like boys."

"No, Annie, we can't go back," Jack whispered.

Heart-of-the-Wind looked thoughtful, and then slowly she nodded. "Yes. I believe words from Jack might help my father think a new thought," she said.

"Great!" said Annie.

"Annie, we can't go back," Jack said again. "What if he won't listen to me? What if he's convinced I was sent here to be the Great Sun of Palenque?"

"Don't worry. You and I don't have to go back," said Annie. "And her father _will_ listen to you. Because it's going to seem like a miracle to him."

"What?" said Jack. "How?"

"Give me the bag, please," said Annie.

Jack handed her their bag. Annie unzipped it. She reached in and pulled out their cell phone.

"*This* will go back with Heart-of-the-Wind," Annie said to Jack, "with an important message from *you*."

CHAPTER NINE

Message for the King

"You are a genius," Jack said to Annie.

She smiled. "Thanks. You probably would have come up with the same plan sooner or later."

"I don't think so," said Jack. "This might be the coolest idea you've ever had."

Annie turned to Heart-of-the-Wind. "This is for you," she said, holding out the cell phone. "Watch." She pressed the "on/off" button and the phone lit up.

"Oh!" Heart-of-the-Wind jumped back.

Jack laughed. "Don't worry, it won't hurt you.

We'll use it to send a message from me to your father."

Heart-of-the-Wind looked puzzled and curious at the same time. Keeping her distance from the phone, she said, "But what is it? Where did it come from?"

"It's a device that . . . well . . . someone named Alexander Graham Bell invented the telephone," said Jack. "Telephones used poles and wires. But then people invented digital phones and wireless communications and satellites and—"

"Stop, Jack," said Annie, interrupting. "We can't go into all that now."

"Right, just watch," Jack said to Heart-of-the-Wind.

"And listen carefully," Annie said.

The Mayan girl nodded, still looking puzzled.

"Ready?" Annie asked Jack.

"Is it charged enough?" he said.

"It should be good for today," said Annie.

"Great," said Jack.

"Think about what you want to say to the

Great Sun of Palenque," said Annie. She tapped the "photos" icon on the screen. Then she held the phone in front of Jack. She tapped the "video camera" icon. "Whenever you're ready," she said.

Jack put down the swim bag, sat on a rock, and thought for a moment. Then he cleared his throat. "Roll camera," he said.

"Right," said Annie. "Action!" Then she pressed "record."

Looking straight at the phone, Jack spoke in a deep, serious voice:

"Greetings, Great Sun of Palenque. I have a message for you. My sister and I have come from Frog Creek, a land far away, to tell you this: women can lead just as well as men. Many women are leaders in our world. They are presidents, queens, senators, school principals, and military leaders. They are just as smart and brave and responsible as our men. That is why you already have the perfect heir to your throne: your daughter Heart-of-the-Wind. She has wisdom and courage far beyond most people, and she will be a

great leader in times of danger and times of peace.
Trust this message from a distant time and place.
Trust your daughter, Heart-of-the-Wind."

Jack stopped speaking and stared intently at the phone.

"Brilliant!" exclaimed Annie after she clicked off the camera. Then she turned to Heart-of-the-Wind. "How did that sound to you?"

"It . . . it was wonderful," said Heart-of-the-Wind. "I only wish my father could have been here to hear it."

"Don't worry," said Annie, smiling. "Watch."

She held up the cell phone so Heart-of-the-Wind could see the screen, and then she pressed "play." Jack's face appeared. *"Greetings, Great Sun of Palenque. . . ."*

Heart-of-the-Wind gasped. "Ohhh! How—how does that happen?"

"It's too hard to explain," said Jack.

"But here's all you have to do," Annie said. "After we go, show this to your father and his warriors. You must do this today. Once the sun goes down, the message can never be seen again. Do you understand?"

"Yes . . . yes," the girl said, nodding.

"Good," said Annie. "So you press *this* button . . . then tap *this* . . . then tap *that*. . . . Easy, right? Try it."

Heart-of-the-Wind cautiously pushed the button and tapped the icons, and Jack's image appeared again. *"Greetings, Great Sun of Palenque. . . ."* Heart-of-the-Wind watched Jack deliver his whole message. When the message was over, she kept looking at the screen in speechless wonder.

"Do you think your father will believe me?" said Jack.

The girl nodded slowly. "Yes . . . yes." She took a deep breath. "He will think this is a great miracle."

"Good! Then we leave it with you," said Annie. "Try not to drop it or get it wet."

"Thank you," Heart-of-the-Wind said, bowing her head.

"We'd better go now," said Jack. "Before anyone discovers we're not in the House of Columns."

"Yes. The sun is rising," Heart-of-the-Wind said. She looked up at the cliff. "The watchmen have left."

"Come on, we have to find our raft," said Jack. As they walked over the cool sand, the mist slowly lifted. In the rosy dawn, a flock of seagulls cried out. They hovered and glided above the waves. The water was sparkling with early light.

"There's the raft!" said Annie. She broke into a run. Heart-of-the-Wind and Jack followed close behind her. When she reached the raft, Annie fell to her knees and felt around in the sand. "It's here, Jack!" she cried, holding up the coin purse. "I found it!"

"Great!" said Jack. "Is the last gold coin still there?"

Annie opened the little purse and looked inside. "Yes! *Everything* is still here—the last coin and all our money! We can go home!" She jumped to her feet.

Jack sighed with relief, and then turned to Heart-of-the-Wind. "Good luck with the message for your father," he said.

The girl pointed to their raft. "Is that how you came here from across the sea?" she asked, looking surprised. "Where is your paddle?"

Annie laughed. "We don't have a paddle," she said. "A shark came after us and—"

"A shark?" interrupted Heart-of-the-Wind, her eyes wide. "A friendly shark?"

"I didn't know there *were* friendly sharks," said Jack.

"Oh, yes. There are many," said Heart-of-the-Wind.

Boy, she's not afraid of anything, thought Jack.

"Well, this one had big teeth," said Annie.

"And it wasn't smiling," said Jack.

"Too bad . . . ," said Heart-of-the-Wind.

"Anyway, the shark attacked our paddle," said Annie. "But we used a special gold coin that our friends gave us, and we made a wish with it, and the raft magically brought us here."

The Mayan girl just nodded.

I guess it takes a lot to shock a girl who talks to jaguars and walking trees, thought Jack.

"So you will use your last gold coin to help you across the sea?" asked Heart-of-the-Wind.

"We will," said Annie.

"And what will you wish for?" asked the girl.

"We'll wish for a safe trip back to Cozumel," said Jack.

"A safe and *fun* trip," said Annie. "The magic only works if we wish to have a wonderful time—that's what our friends wanted."

Annie reached into the purse, took out the gold coin, and put the purse back in their bag. "You want to watch us leave?" she asked.

"Oh, yes," said Heart-of-the-Wind.

"Let's get this in the water first," said Jack. He set their bag on top of the raft. Then he and Annie pushed the raft across the sand into the shallow water. As Heart-of-the-Wind watched from the shore, Jack and Annie climbed aboard.

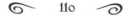

By now, the sky was orange and red. The sun was rising in the east. Annie held up the gold coin. It glittered in the dawn light.

"Wait!" said Heart-of-the-Wind. "May I make the wish for you?"

"I think we'd better do it ourselves," said Jack.

"Oh, she can do it," said Annie.

"But—" said Jack.

"Oh, come on, let her try," said Annie.

"Okay," said Jack, sighing.

Heart-of-the-Wind waded into the water, and Annie handed her the gold coin. "All you have to do is wish for us to have a safe, fun trip to Cozumel. Then toss the coin into the air. Got it?"

"Yes," said the Mayan girl. "I will give you a miracle, like you gave to me." She tightened her fist around the coin. She whispered something, and then tossed the coin high into the air.

The gold coin burst into the most radiant display yet—tiny purple, green, blue, and yellow sparks flew into the sky, vanishing into the bright dawn.

"She whispered something, and then tossed the coin high into the air."

"Thanks! Good—" Before Jack could say *bye,* the raft shot across the water into the blinding orange-red sunrise.

"Bye! Bye!" Jack and Annie called.

Heart-of-the-Wind was laughing and waving.

"Good luck with your future!" Jack called.

The girl at the edge of the sea grew smaller as the raft headed east, gliding over the calm water. When they couldn't see Heart-of-the-Wind anymore, Jack sat back and relaxed. He looked up at the sky. Gulls were circling lazily overhead. The sky was deep blue now.

"I hope you don't mind that we had to leave our cell phone behind," Annie said.

"Not at all," said Jack. "I'm not a big cell phone user. We can tell Mom and Dad we're sorry we left our phone . . ."

"By the water," Annie finished.

"And that's the truth," said Jack, smiling. As he felt sea spray and the warmth of the rising sun on his face, the seagulls began to screech overhead.

Jack looked up again: all the gulls were dipping up and down in the sky, shrieking and flapping. "What's wrong with them?" he asked.

Annie gasped. "Oh, no! Look!" she cried, pointing behind them.

"What?" said Jack.

"That! *That!*" shouted Annie, waving her finger.

Jack couldn't believe his eyes.

A huge shark fin was moving across the water, heading for their raft.

CHAPTER TEN

Into the Dawn

"Not again!" Jack cried. "Didn't Heart-of-the-Wind wish for a *safe* ride?"

"I don't know!" said Annie. "I thought I made it clear!"

The shark fin sliced through the sea, following the swiftly moving raft.

Jack didn't know what to do. They'd used their last coin! He stared in shock at the huge fin. Though the shark seemed to be keeping its distance, it swam steadily after the raft.

"Maybe he won't attack!" said Annie.

Annie had barely said these words before the shark shot forward, its humongous body rising above the surface of the sea. It was as big as a whale! Its brown skin was speckled with white spots. It had a flattened head with a blunt snout and a huge mouth at least five feet wide!

The shark dipped under the raft! Then the raft was lifted into the air and held aloft. The raft was sitting on the back of the shark!

"AHHHH!" screamed Jack and Annie. They grabbed each other and held on tightly. As the raft teetered back and forth on the shark's back, Jack expected to be hurled into the waves. He closed his eyes, waiting for the worst.

But nothing bad happened. The raft kept going, and the wind kept blowing.

"Open your eyes, Jack!" Annie said.

Jack opened his eyes. Swimming close to the surface of the water, the shark perfectly balanced the raft on its back.

"What is he doing?" said Jack.

"I don't know!" shouted Annie. "Maybe he's

taking us to Cozumel! Maybe that's what Heart-of-the-Wind wished for!"

"What?" cried Jack.

"For a shark to help us have a fun, safe ride!" shouted Annie.

"That's crazy!" cried Jack.

"It's wonderful!" said Annie.

Wonderful? thought Jack. *Riding on the back of a monster shark?*

"I'll bet he's a *friendly* shark!" cried Annie. "Look up sharks in the travel guide!"

"Oh, brother," said Jack. But as the shark gently carried them across the waves, he reached into the bag and pulled out their travel guide. With the wind whipping the pages, he looked in the index for *shark*. His eyes caught two words: *shark, whale.*

"Whale shark! That's it!" Jack shouted. He found the right page and read aloud:

> **The whale shark is the biggest fish in the world. Every year, hundreds of these**

gigantic creatures migrate to waters off the Yucatán. Whale sharks eat only sea plants and fish and do not harm people. In fact, sometimes these gentle giants allow divers to hitch a ride.

"See! I told you!" cried Annie. "Whale sharks don't harm people. This is the miracle Heart-of-the-Wind wanted to give us!"

Holding the raft on his back, the giant shark kept swimming across the Caribbean, heading into the light of the sunrise.

Overhead, seagulls, terns, and pelicans careened and cawed raucously. They seemed to be laughing at the shark swimming with the raft on his back. Jack began to relax and enjoy himself. The nutty seabirds, the salty air, and the giant shark's speedy rolling motion through the water, rising and falling with the waves, made the ride extra spectacular. Jack wanted it to last forever.

"Land ho!" Annie shouted.

"Swimming close to the surface of the water, the shark perfectly balanced the raft on its back."

Jack shaded his eyes and squinted at the horizon. In the distance he could see Cozumel—the sugary-white sand, the stone pyramid, and the palm trees.

When they drew close to shore, the shark dipped lower in the water, leaving the raft floating on the surface for a moment. Then the raft began skimming across the sea on its own, heading for the beach, until finally it came to rest on the hard, wet sand.

Jack and Annie jumped off and looked back at the water. They saw the huge fin moving out to sea.

"Bye! Thanks!" Annie shouted, waving.

The whale shark's fin vanished into the sparkling horizon.

Neither Jack nor Annie spoke for a moment. Then Jack heaved a sigh. Exhausted, sunburned, and salty from sea spray, he put the damp travel guide into the bag. He handed Annie her flip-flops, and he put his on, too. Then he slung the bag over his shoulder. "Ready?"

"Ready," said Annie.

They walked through the warm sand to the palm tree with the rope ladder. Annie climbed up first, and Jack followed.

Inside the tree house, a breeze rustled the palm leaves. Jack picked up the Pennsylvania book. "Ready?" he said again.

Annie stood at the window, looking out at the turquoise-blue sea. She turned to Jack with a big grin. "That was some vacation," she said.

"Yep. Some vacation," Jack agreed. He shook his head in wonder and then pointed at a picture of the Frog Creek woods. "I wish we could go there."

The wind started to blow.

The tree house started to spin.

It spun faster and faster.

Then everything was still.

Absolutely still.

☀ ☀ ☀

A breeze blew into the tree house. Jack smelled summer leaves and pine needles. "Ah, home," he said.

"Home," said Annie, smiling. "It's always nice to come home after a vacation."

"But did you have a good time?" said a voice from nearby.

"Teddy!" Jack and Annie said together.

"I thought I'd come back to welcome you home." The young sorcerer was sitting on a limb of the oak tree. Holding on to the branch, he climbed nimbly through the tree house window. "So. Did you? Have a good time?" he said.

"Yes!" said Annie. "The best!"

"Even though it wasn't exactly what we expected," said Jack.

"What happened? Did your snorkel equipment not work properly?" said Teddy.

"No, our gear was fine. What surprised us was the shark attack," said Jack.

"And being captured by ancient Mayan warriors," said Annie.

"And escaping through a swampy forest," said Jack.

"And then traveling through the Underworld, where the ancestor spirits live," said Annie.

"And almost becoming the next Great Sun of Palenque," said Jack.

"I see ... ," said Teddy. "But other than that, you had fun?"

Jack and Annie laughed.

"Seriously, what happened?" asked Teddy.

"Seriously, what we just said is *exactly* what happened," said Annie.

"Let me explain," said Jack. He unzipped their swim bag, pulled out their travel guide, and pointed to the illustration of the pyramid on the cover. "By pointing to *this* picture, we went back to *ancient* Mexico—like Mexico more than a thousand years ago."

"Ah, I see ... ," said Teddy. "So no luxury spa hotels?"

"Nope," said Jack.

"But with help from your magic coins, everything worked out fine," said Annie. "We actually

had a really great time, and we think we might have helped a Mayan girl become the ruler of her people."

"Really?" said Teddy.

"Really. *And* we hitched a ride on the back of the biggest shark on the planet," said Jack.

"Literally," said Annie. "We used all your coins to have fun."

"Speaking of that, you can have your coin purse back," said Jack. He reached again into the swim bag and took out the small velvet purse. Before he handed it to Teddy, he opened it. All the fifty-dollar bills were gone. "It's empty!" he said.

Annie shrugged. "I guess the money was only meant for our vacation, and it turns out we didn't need money at all."

Jack laughed. "Easy come, easy go," he said. He gave the coin purse to Teddy, and Annie handed over the travel guide.

"You must tell me more of the story sometime," said Teddy.

"We will. But right now we should head home," said Jack. He felt a little homesick. It was probably because they had talked to Heart-of-the-Wind about missing their parents.

"Please thank Morgan and Merlin for our dream vacation," said Annie.

"Indeed," said Teddy. "Perhaps they will send you on another one soon."

"Not *too* soon, I hope," said Annie. "We need to recover from this one first."

"Yeah, we need a vacation from our vacation," said Jack.

Teddy laughed.

Jack picked up their swim bag and started down the rope ladder. Annie followed. Teddy was looking out the window when they reached the ground. "Good-bye!" he called. "I hope to see you again in these woods!"

A blinding light swirled upward around the trunk of the oak—and in a flash, the magic tree house was gone.

"Good-bye," Annie said softly.

"Home," said Jack. He strapped the bag onto his bike rack. Then he and Annie climbed on their bicycles and headed down the rough path between the trees. They bumped over roots and fallen bark and pine needles, until they came out of the Frog Creek woods and onto their street. Then they pedaled to their house.

Jack and Annie parked their bikes in the garage and headed up to their porch.

"Mom! Dad!" Annie shouted as they went through the front door. "We're back from snorkeling!"

"Come tell us all about it!" their dad called from the kitchen.

"And have some pizza!" said their mom. "It just came out of the oven."

"Thanks! Be right there!" said Jack. "We have to check something real fast."

"What are we checking?" Annie asked as she followed him into the living room.

"Something online," said Jack. He sat down at

the computer and typed the search words *Mayan ruler, Heart-of-the-Wind.*

An entry popped up immediately. Jack clicked on it, then read aloud:

> **Yohl Ik'nal was the ruler of the Mayan city of Palenque from 583 to 604. Her name means "Heart of the Wind."**

"Ohhh! YAY!" said Annie.
"Wait," said Jack. He read on:

> **She became queen after the death of her father, the Great Sun of Palenque. She was the first female ruler in recorded Mayan history. She must have come to the throne due to extremely unusual circumstances, the details of which have not survived.**

Jack and Annie looked at each other. "That is *so* cool," Annie whispered with awe.

"I guess a cell phone message from a kid more than a thousand years in the future could be considered an unusual circumstance," said Jack.

"Yep. Extremely," said Annie.

Jack smiled and shut down the computer. "I'm starving," he said. "Let's get some pizza."

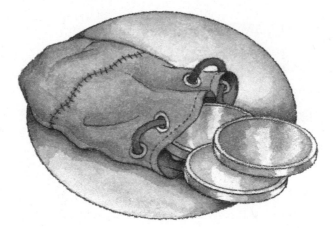

Turn the page for a sneak peek at
Magic Tree House Fact Tracker:
Sharks and Other Predators

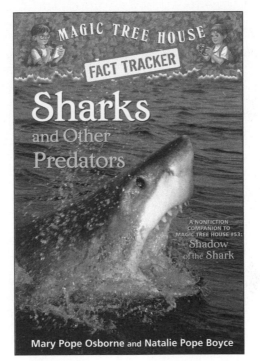

Megalodon—Yikes!

Scientists usually learn about early animals by studying fossils of their skeletons. Shark cartilage often dissolves before the skeletons can become fossils. Sharks' teeth are made from a hard mineral, not cartilage. The best fossils of ancient sharks are their teeth.

Some of these teeth are more than twice as big as a great white's! They belonged to a gigantic shark called *Megalodon* (MEG-uh-luh-don), which lived millions of years ago. These gigantic creatures were probably over sixty feet long with mouths seven feet wide. That's one big old predator!

*Megalodon*s were large enough to eat whales. They might have eaten about 2,500 pounds of food a day! And these sharks were everywhere, in oceans around the world.

Mystery: Who Killed the Great White?

In 2003, scientists in Australia tagged a nine-foot great white shark. The tag was to record how deep it swam and what its temperature was.

Sometime later, the tag without the shark washed up on an Australian beach. It showed that the shark had been 1,900 feet down in the ocean. It also said that the temperature had been forty-six degrees. But then it suddenly shot up to seventy-eight degrees. It stayed that way for eight days.

Scientists now think that a larger animal dragged the shark down in the cold deep ocean. The high temperature was from inside its attacker's stomach.

What animal is big enough to eat a nine-foot shark? What animal's stomach is around seventy-eight degrees? Experts are pretty sure the predator was a killer whale!